Three Gifts For Abigail

Allison Romero

Illustrations by Gloria Elliott

A Grackle Book

Grackle Publishing - Ambler, Pennsylvania

Grackle
An imprint of Grackle Publishing, LLC
gracklepublishing.com

For Abigail

Abigail felt the warm sun on her face and blinked her eyes open.

Remembering what day it was, she smiled, jumped out of bed, and ran downstairs. She paused on the landing of the stairs and peered over the balcony into the living room.

Just like every Easter before, there sat her yellow wicker Easter basket on the living room table.

"Good morning, Abigail." Her mommy smiled.

Abigail smiled back and ran down the last few steps to her basket. She picked it up and cuddled next to her mommy on the couch as her daddy picked up his Bible.

"Do you know what today is, Abigail?" her daddy began.

"Easter!"

"That's right. Today, I'm going to tell you about the whole Easter story. It started a long, long time ago in a place called the Garden of Eden."

"In the beginning, when God created everything, He also created a man and a woman named Adam and Eve. God gave them everything they could want and need in the Garden of Eden. He just gave them one rule, to not eat from the special tree. But, Adam and Eve didn't listen."

Daddy opened his bible to Genesis 3:6:

> When the woman saw that the fruit of the tree was good for food and pleasing to the eye, and also desirable for gaining wisdom, she took some and ate it. She also gave some to her husband, who was with her, and he ate it.

Daddy looked at Abigail. "Were they supposed to eat that fruit, Abigail?"

Abigail shook her head. "No, they disobeyed."

"That's right," Daddy continued, "and because they disobeyed, they brought sin into the world. Now we all sin and we all deserve to be punished. But, God made a promise. He promised that He would send a savior to save everyone from their sins. And he did. Do you know who that savior is, Abigail?"

"Jesus!" Abigail shouted excitedly, knowing the story by heart.

"That's right!"

Daddy flipped through his Bible to John 3:16:

> For God so loved the world that he gave his one and only Son,
> that whoever believes in him shall not perish but have eternal life.

"Jesus taught everyone he could about this good news. He taught them about God and how to live. But, some people didn't like that. Instead of believing in Jesus, they hung him on the cross to die."

Again daddy flipped through his Bible, this time to Matthew 27:29-31:

> and then [they] twisted together a crown of thorns and set it on his head. They put a staff in his right hand. Then they knelt in front of him and mocked him. "Hail, king of the Jews!" they said. They spit on him, and took the staff and struck him on the head again and again. After they had mocked him, they took off the robe and put his own clothes on him. Then they led him away to crucify him.

Abigail felt sad as she pulled out the first item in her Easter basket.

"And that's why the first item in your basket is a cross," Abigail's mommy began. "It's a reminder not only of what Jesus did for you, but also that God keeps his promises."

"Although we can be sad about the way Jesus was treated," Daddy continued, "we don't have to stay sad. Let's read what happened next."

He flipped through his Bible once more until he landed on a passage from Matthew 27:66:

> So they went and made the tomb secure by putting a seal on the stone and posting the guard.

"This passage tells us that after Jesus died, his friends buried him in a tomb with a big stone in front. But, that's not the end of the story."

Abigail pulled the second item out of her basket and rubbed the smooth gemstone knowing what happened next.

"After three days, this is what happened." Daddy read from the bible once more. Matthew 28:2-7:

> There was a violent earthquake, for an angel of the Lord came down from heaven and, going to the tomb, rolled back the stone and sat on it.
>
> His appearance was like lightning, and his clothes were white as snow. The guards were so afraid of him that they shook and became like dead men. The angel said to the women, "Do not be afraid, for I know that you are looking for Jesus, who was crucified. He is not here; he has risen, just as he said. Come and see the place where he lay. Then go quickly and tell his disciples: 'He has risen from the dead and is going ahead of you into Galilee. There you will see him.'"

"Did Jesus stay dead, Abigail?"

"No, he came alive again!"

Abigail's heart pounded with excitement as she studied the gemstone. Every year a new and beautiful gemstone appeared in her basket. This one was a bright green oval that shimmered in the sun.

"That's right. The second item in your basket is a gemstone. It reminds you of the stone that was rolled away when Jesus rose again."

11

"After Jesus rose from the dead, he went to visit with his friends. First, he visited with Mary and other women in the garden. Then, he visited with his disciples. Eventually, he saw over five-hundred people and gave them this message."

Daddy flipped to the last passage and read what Jesus said from Matthew 28:19-20:

> "Therefore go and make disciples of all nations, baptizing them in the name of the Father and of the Son and of the Holy Spirit, and teaching them to obey everything I have commanded you. And surely I am with you always, to the very end of the age."

Finally, at the best part, Abigail grabbed a handful of candy out of the basket.

"The third gift in your basket," Mommy gently reminded Abigail, "is to remind you to share with others the good news of Jesus and salvation. Just as you're going to share your candy with others, Jesus wants you to share the Easter story so that everyone can enjoy what you get to enjoy."

Abigail looked through the handful of candy and picked out the best pieces to share with her cousins later in the day.

She stopped as a thought popped into her head. "The story says that anyone who believes in Jesus will be saved."

Mommy nodded. "That's right, Abigail."

"How does he know?"

"Know what?"

Abigail looked up at Daddy. "Know that I believe."

Daddy folded his hands. "That's a good question, Abigail. All we have to do is tell him. You can pray and tell Jesus you're sorry for your sins and you'd like to accept him and believe in him as your savior."

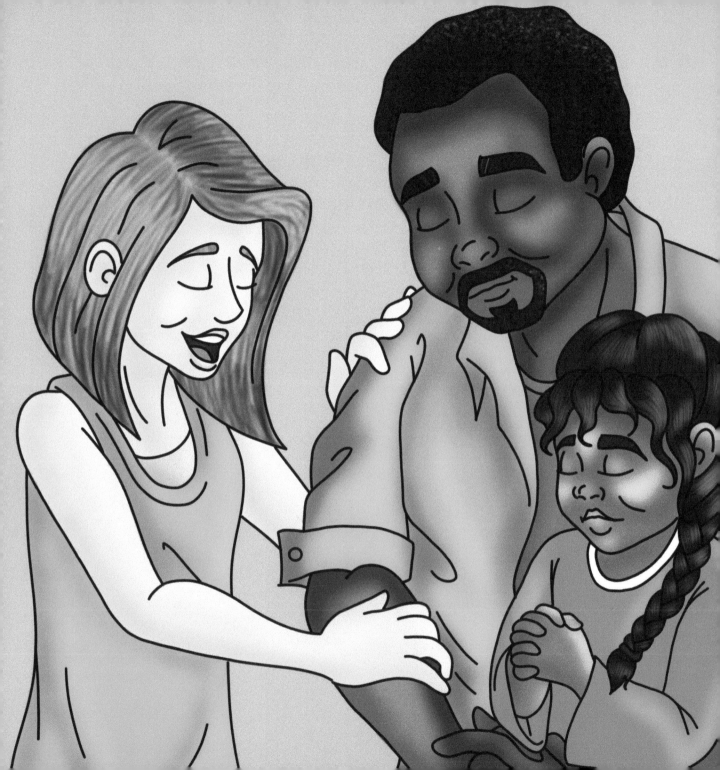

Abigail thought for a moment.

Mommy smiled. "Would you like to do that, Abigail?"

Abigail smiled back. "Yes, can you help me?"

Together, Daddy, Mommy, and Abigail folded their hands and Abigail told Jesus how sorry she was for the things she did wrong and promised to try her best to do better. She thanked him for coming to save her and asked him to stay with her forever.

After she finished her prayer, Mommy and Daddy gave her big hugs.

Daddy sat back down and closed his Bible.

"And that," he said, "is the Easter story."

A Grackle Book

CPSIA information can be obtained
at www.ICGtesting.com
Printed in the USA
BVHW021417171120
593515BV00015B/1217